SPACE SCOUT ™

SCOUTING THE UNIVERSE FOR A NEW EARTH

The Big Freeze
published in 2010 by
Hardie Grant Egmont
85 High Street
Prahran, Victoria 3181, Australia
www.hardiegrantegmont.com.au

Hardie Grant Egmont uses
Greenhouse Friendly™
ENVI Carbon Neutral Paper

CONSUMER   ENVI Carbon Neutral Paper is an Australian Government
certified Greenhouse Friendly™ Product.

The text for this book has been printed on ENVI Carbon Neutral Paper.

A CiP record for this title is available from the National Library of Australia

Cover illustration by D. Mackie
Illustrated by C. Bennett and A. Mackie
Design by S. Swingler
Typeset by Ektavo
Printed in Australia by McPherson's Printing Group

1 3 5 7 9 10 8 6 4 2

SPACE™
SCOUT

THE BIG FREEZE

BY **H. BADGER**

ILLUSTRATED BY **C. BENNETT** AND **A. MACKIE**

hardie grant EGMONT

CHAPTER 1

It was the year 2354, and Kip Kirby was busy packing for a trip to space.

'Got your portable meteorite detector?' his dad asked.

'Check,' said Kip, patting his backpack.

'Powdered broccoli?'

'Packed it, Mum,' Kip replied, trying not to gag.

Kip wished his parents would relax, but that wasn't going to happen. Not when Kip was starting work as a WorldCorp Space Scout today.

WorldCorp was the only corporation left on Earth. It was all-powerful. WorldCorp hired Space Scouts to search for a planet that could become Earth 2.

They needed a new planet because there were over a trillion people on Earth — they were running out of room!

There were 49 Space Scouts already searching the galaxies. Every Space Scout wanted to find the perfect planet first.

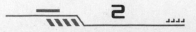

'I'm so proud WorldCorp picked you,' sniffled Kip's mum. 'The youngest ever Space Scout!' She took a SnotSucker from her pocket. SnotSuckers automatically sucked the snot from your nose without you needing to blow.

Kip tried not to roll his eyes. Instead, he glanced at his pet minisaur Duke, who lay basking in the sun on the carpet. Minisaurs were knee-high brontosauruses. They were bred as pets from fossil DNA.

Sometimes wilful and difficult to train

Friendly and playful

40cm
30cm
20cm
10cm
0cm

WorldCorp Minisaur: Duke

Slightly larger than a domestic cat

Being cold-blooded, Duke basked as often as he could. It was how he got energy.

Scratching Duke's scaly head, Kip gazed out of his bedroom window on the 2,342nd floor of his building.

Earth was so crowded that apartment buildings were thousands of storeys high. There was no room for back yards or swimming pools.

Suddenly, there was a loud beep. It was the alarm on Kip's SpaceCuff, telling him it was time to leave.

The SpaceCuff was an essential piece of Space Scout gear. It was a thick silver wristband, and had an in-built computer for communicating. There was even a

Cuff automatically adjusts to wearer's arm

Holographic projector

Camera for visual communication

WorldCorp SpaceCuff

laser pocket-knife function.

'I'd better go,' Kip said to his parents, his excitement rising. After three months of Space Scout training, Kip couldn't wait to leave Earth for his first mission.

A nervous look crossed his mum's face.

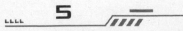

NAME: KIP KIRBY

AGE: 12 years and 3 months. This is 8 years younger than any other Space Scout. WorldCorp has made an exception because of Kirby's impressive skills and love of risk-taking

LOOKS: Brown hair, hazel eyes – innocent look will not threaten aliens

INTELLIGENCE: High, but has not reached dangerous nerd level

STRENGTH: Good genes from athletic parents

ICE-CREAM FLAVOUR: Choc-Cicada Crunch – suggests adventurous personality

PETS: Minisaur called Duke

SCHOOL: 23 choir rehearsals missed – excuses show creativity and pluck

Made with 100% biodegradable resin

FACT FILE

'I'll be fine, Mum. I've got the skills I need,' said Kip. 'Otherwise WorldCorp wouldn't have picked me.'

Kip grabbed his helmet and smoothed his green spacesuit. The gleaming heat-proof suit fit him perfectly.

Kip and his parents stepped into the lift in their apartment. The lift shot 1,158 floors to the roof of the building in 0.2 seconds. It was just enough time to see one of WorldCorp's super-fast MicroAds on the lift's 3D TV.

The circular lift doors opened. A WorldCorp UniTaxi sat on a launch pad in the middle of the roof. Shaped like a jellybean, the UniTaxi was green with a clear roof. As Kip walked towards the taxi, its door automatically slid open. He hugged his parents goodbye and quickly got

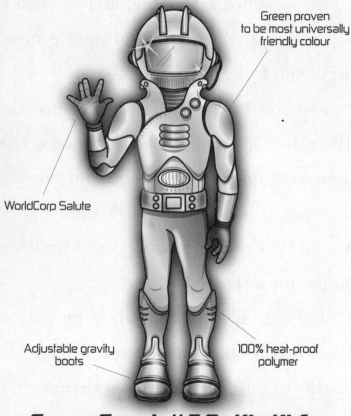

Green proven to be most universally friendly colour

WorldCorp Salute

Adjustable gravity boots

100% heat-proof polymer

Space Scout #50: Kip Kirby

into the taxi before his mum got teary.

Time to grow up…or at least act that way,
Kip thought.

Kip was a Space Scout now. He couldn't
have his parents freaking out just because
this was his first solo trip into space.

Kip settled into the taxi, his backpack at
his feet. He put on his helmet. Underneath
him, the UniTaxi's algae-powered engine
purred.

Kip checked the Intergalactic Positioning
System on the UniTaxi's trip computer.

DESTINATION:
Intergalactic Hoverport

ASSIGNED TRANSPORT:
Starship MoNa 4000

Kip couldn't believe he was about to take off on his first Space Scout mission. It would have been a perfect moment, except for one thing. Since Kip was younger than the other Space Scouts, WorldCorp had decided he needed a second-in-command on his missions, or a 2iC for short.

A calm, wise and knowledgeable individual. That's how WorldCorp had described his 2iC back in Space Scout training.

Yuck, Kip thought. *Sounds like one of my Teacherbots from school!*

CHAPTER 2

The UniTaxi shot into the air, slamming Kip back into his seat. It was on auto-pilot, and was programmed to fly Kip to the Intergalactic Hoverport.

The Hoverport hovered high in the sky, 10 kilometres into Earth's atmosphere. All space-craft travelling long distances left from the Hoverport.

All kinds of ships were docked there, mostly for short trips to Mars and Venus.

As the UniTaxi sped away from Earth, Kip turned around to check out the view.

He thought about the first time he'd been to space. He'd gone on a family holiday to Venus. *Bit of a dud holiday*, he remembered. *It was too hot to take off our heat-proof spacesuits.*

All the solar system's planets were too hot, too cold or too gassy to replace Earth. Finding another planet for humans meant searching way beyond the Milky Way galaxy. And only Space Scouts were allowed to travel that far.

Kip turned back and looked through

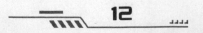

the UniTaxi's windscreen.
He couldn't see them yet,
but there were zillions of
planets to explore out there.

It's a big job, Kip thought. *But I'll show WorldCorp I can do it. And I'll prove I don't need a 2iC!*

The UniTaxi whizzed into the Hover-port, which looked like a gigantic floating carpark.

Kip spotted his ship, MoNa 4000. It was designed especially for high-speed, long-distance space travel.

MoNa was glossy black and had curved thrusters. Two narrow windows glowed like eyes over her nose cone.

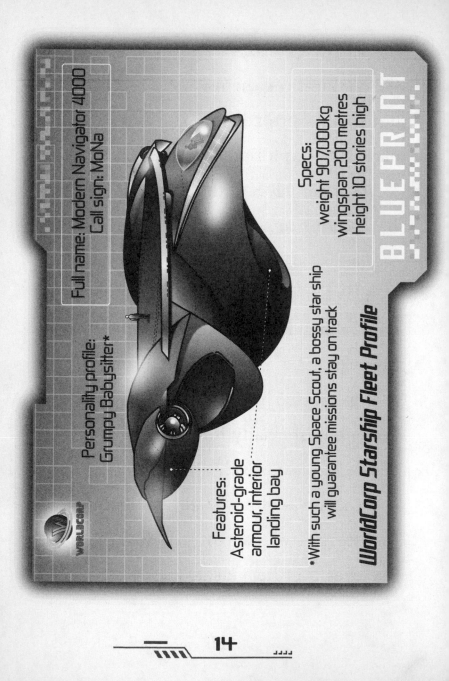

BLUEPRINT

Full name: Modern Navigator 4000
Call sign: MoNa

Specs:
weight 907,000kg
wingspan 200 metres
height 10 stories high

Personality profile:
Grumpy Babysitter*

Features:
Asteroid-grade
armour, interior
landing bay

*With such a young Space Scout, a bossy star ship
will guarantee missions stay on track

WORLDCORP

WorldCorp Starship Fleet Profile

Kip's UniTaxi flew towards MoNa. A hatch slid open underneath the ship's nose. Inside, Kip saw a landing bay.

Suddenly, a bossy voice sounded from Kip's SpaceCuff.

'MoNa to Kip Kirby,' said the voice. 'Technical issues with my landing beacon. I can't guide your UniTaxi in to land automatically.'

'That's OK,' said Kip, his hands shaking just a bit. 'I'll land it myself.'

Stay cool, Kip told himself. *Look it up in your MindFiles!*

Kip sorted through his MindFiles. These computer programs had been installed directly into his brain during

Space Scout training. The files contained vital information to use on missions.

The UniTaxi sped closer and closer to MoNa. If Kip didn't find the right MindFile, he was going to crash!

Essentials of Landing High-Powered Space-Craft... that sounded right.

Kip secured his safety harness. He looked on the UniTaxi's holographic dashboard for the Auto-Pilot Override button, pressing the first button he found.

The space junk wipers switched on.

Oops, wrong button, Kip thought.

'Sure you're up to this?' asked MoNa.

'One hundred per cent sure,' Kip said, quickly pressing another button.

This time, the screen flashed and the taxi wheels lowered.

```
WorldCorp UniTaxi
AUTO-PILOT OVERRIDE
```

Now I steer towards the landing bay, he thought. *Easy!*

But the UniTaxi's steering was so heavy! Kip could hardly control it.

The UniTaxi dipped lower.

Crouching on his seat, Kip used all his body weight to pull the joystick up.

The UniTaxi's nose lifted up just in time. Kip was going to make it! The tyres skidded across the landing bay.

Not perfect, Kip admitted. *But at least my*

2iC didn't see…

Kip's mouth dropped open. He stared through the windscreen, goggle-eyed.

Standing in the landing bay was a giant, walking furball.

The creature was two metres tall with shaggy white fur, ice-blue eyes and pointed fangs.

Cautiously, Kip stepped out of the taxi.

'Welcome, Kip,' said the creature, wagging its tail. 'I'm Finbar, your second-in-command.'

Kip shook Finbar's paw.

'Take off your helmet if you like,' said Finbar. 'MoNa's air is safe to breathe.'

Kip pulled his helmet off and tucked it

under his arm.

'I'll show you around,' Finbar said. 'On the top floor, there's the zero-gravity games room. We sleep in harnesses mounted to the wall, and —'

'This is a Space Scout mission, not a holiday camp,' snapped MoNa, her voice echoing around them.

'She hears everything we say,' Finbar whispered.

That's just great, Kip thought. *On top of saving Earth, I've got a giant wolf and a nosy starship to deal with as well!*

CHAPTER 3

'Your mission brief is ready,' said MoNa. 'Report immediately to the bridge.'

As on all starships, MoNa's control centre was called the bridge.

Hang on, thought Kip, *aren't I captain of this ship?*

But Kip didn't want to annoy MoNa so early in the mission. Even though he hated

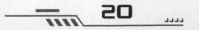

being bossed around, he followed Finbar out of the landing bay.

Kip and Finbar walked down a glowing blue corridor. Hundreds of round portholes were set into the walls, floor and ceiling. Through them, Kip could see the black sky flecked with stars.

MoNa had already left the Hoverport and auto-piloted out of Earth's atmosphere. They were now in outer space.

'So, why the emergency landing?' asked Finbar as they walked. 'MoNa's landing beacon isn't broken.'

MoNa was testing me! thought Kip.

Every door Kip and Finbar came to slid open automatically. Behind each door were more corridors heading in every direction.

'How do you find your way around?' asked Kip.

'It's easy because I'm an Animaul,' said Finbar. 'Part-human, part-wolf.'

Kip stopped in his tracks. He'd heard of Animauls, of course. He'd just never been sure they really existed.

Animauls were another WorldCorp invention. They were humans crossed with vicious animals such as wolves, pythons and crocodiles.

The kids at school said they were created

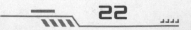

to protect Earth in case of alien invasion.

'Don't be scared,' snorted MoNa. 'Finbar failed Animaul basic training. He's too friendly!'

Finbar looked as sheepish as a giant wolf-man could. 'I was reassigned here when you started as a Space Scout,' he explained to Kip.

'When they decided I need a 2iC,' Kip said, scowling.

'Not that WorldCorp thought you couldn't do the job,' Finbar said quickly. 'They thought you'd find my wolfish sense of direction and loyalty helpful. Plus, I guard MoNa when she's docked at the Hoverport.'

All Space Scout starships had guards

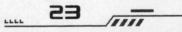

WORLDCORP

ANIMAUL FILE
Name: Finbar
Species: Part-human, part-arctic wolf
Age: 20 years (140 dog years)
Skills: Highly developed sense of direction and smell.
Vision outstanding. Great with languages
Strengths: Calm, wise and caring
Weaknesses: Too kind for his own good

because of the expensive technology on
board. Kip didn't think a failed Animaul
would make the best guard, though.

At least he's not a Teacherbot, Kip decided.
Anyway, Finbar was proving himself useful
already. He had led them straight to the
bridge.

Finbar leant in close to the door leading to the bridge. A blue laser shot out and scanned his eye. Then the door slid open.

The front wall of the bridge was sloping, with huge windows looking out into space. The floor was a map of the known universe that lit up when Kip stepped on it. In the middle of the room were two chairs.

Kip and Finbar sat down. Kip raised his hand and touched the air above him.

Instantly, Kip and Finbar's chairs were surrounded by a blue holographic cylinder. MoNa's controls were projected onto the cylinder.

Kip activated the holographic controls by touching them. He'd learnt how to use

 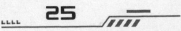

the system in Space Scout training.

'As you know, MoNa can fly herself for ordinary space travel,' said Finbar. 'But she needs you for wormholes.'

SPACE DICTIONARY

Wormhole: A shortcut between galaxies. Wormholes allow starships to travel billions of light years in seconds. Wormholes are dangerous. Only trained Space Scouts can fly through them safely.

DICTIONARY

Using his paw, Finbar scribbled on a holographic writing pad in front of him. Kip read what he had written:

Watch out! MoNa thinks

she can do it all herself.

Kip realised that this was the only way he could talk to Finbar without MoNa

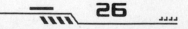

hearing. He nodded at his 2iC.

Just then a message flashed on the holographic consol.

DOWNLOAD MISSION BRIEF

Kip touched the air to download the brief. It appeared on the screen.

**SPACE SCOUT
KIP KIRBY
MISSION BRIEF**

A wormhole to the Mega Meteor Galaxy has opened up. There is a planet of interest there called Eden-7.

Eden-7 has three suns. WorldCorp scientists think the planet will be warm, sunny and good for humans.

Your mission:
Travel through the wormhole, confirm Eden-7's sunny climate, and explore the planet.
Report your findings to WorldCorp.

CLASSIFIED

Kip looked at the universe map on the floor. The wormhole was supposed to be close by. But Kip's stomach was rumbling.

'Before we get going, I might just have a squirt of BurgerMousse,' he said.

BurgerMousse was Kip's favourite canned snack.

'Certainly not,' MoNa snapped. 'My system says the wormhole's only open for a few more minutes.'

Just then Kip heard a loud rumble. The holographic consol flashed a message:

auto mega-drive engaged

MoNa leapt forward. Light flashed. For

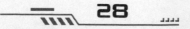

a split second, Kip's brain froze. His skin prickled and his hair stood on end.

'As Space Scout and captain of this starship, I order you to stop,' Kip yelled above the noise.

MoNa laughed.

'Take the controls,' said Finbar urgently. 'If she flies herself into the wormhole, we're in serious trouble.'

But it was too late. MoNa was piloting herself into the wormhole. And she was travelling at ten times the speed of light!

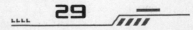

CHAPTER 4

The wormhole loomed up in the window. It was a gigantic mass of swirling clouds. Like a powerful vacuum cleaner, the wormhole sucked MoNa inside.

Kip had the strange sensation of being turned inside out. Green, pink, red and yellow lights exploded all around.

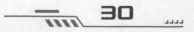

They were spinning. Falling. Fast!

The holographic consol swam before
Kip's eyes. The were upside-down, but
he could just make out a button that read
Auto-Pilot Override.

He touched it. A holographic steering
control panel flashed up on the screen

in front of his captain's chair. He swiped expertly at the controls, swinging MoNa the right way up.

MoNa popped out the other end of the wormhole, like a baked bean and bacon jaffle from an InstaDine vending machine. That had been *waaaaay* too close.

'Never do that again, MoNa,' said Kip sternly.

Silence.

'You might have more space experience than me,' Kip said. 'But I am captain and we've got to work together.'

'I suppose you're right,' said MoNa.

'And?' said Kip.

'I'm sorry,' said MoNa. There was a

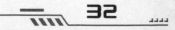

pause. 'But I still know more than you!' she blurted out.

Kip rolled his eyes. MoNa was impossible! But at least he'd proven she couldn't walk all over him.

Kip gazed out the windows in front of him. They were in a whole new galaxy, never before visited by humans.

'Black sky, stars. Just like our galaxy, don't you think?' Kip said to Finbar.

But Finbar's chair was empty.

'What was that?' came Finbar's muffled voice from under his chair.

He crawled out and sat down carefully. 'Wormholes make me nervous,' Finbar explained.

Kip decided to change the subject. He pointed to a nearby planet close to the galaxy's three suns.

'Do you think that's Eden-7?' he asked.

'It's grey and icy,' Finbar said, getting up. 'Isn't Eden-7 supposed to be warm?'

'WorldCorp uploaded Eden-7's likely location,' MoNa chimed in. 'That planet matches the co-ordinates.'

'Must be it,' said Kip. 'Take us closer, MoNa.'

MoNa sped towards Eden-7's atmosphere. Her windows frosted over with thick ice as they passed through. An ugly meteorite crater scarred the planet's

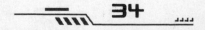

surface. Dust clouds covered everything.

'Approaching destination,' said MoNa. 'Scrambler Beam activated.'

'I hate that thing,' Finbar shuddered. 'It scrambles our particles, beams them through the sky, and rearranges them on our destination planet.'

A beam of light shot down from the roof of the bridge. On the floor below the light, Kip saw a pair of footprints and a pair of pawprints.

Kip did up his spacesuit and put his helmet back on. He attached the hose to an OxyGlobe, which squeezed enough oxygen for two days into a tank as small as a tennis ball.

 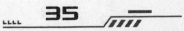

Two days
of oxygen

Strong globe
shape to withstand
massive pressure

WorldCorp OxyGlobe

When Finbar had his spacesuit on, they stood on their footprints under the beam.

There was a soft hum. Kip felt a sharp tingling, like pins and needles all over his body. Then MoNa shot a beam of light down to Eden-7. Kip and Finbar went with it, in millions of tiny pieces.

WHOMP!

Kip's particles reformed on the rocky surface of Eden-7. He was whole again.

The beam had vanished.

Beside him, Finbar whimpered. His spacesuit was specially shaped to fit his ears. That's how Kip knew they were flattened in fear.

WorldCorp had predicted a sunny planet. But when Kip checked the temperature on his SpaceCuff, it was 316 degrees below zero! Freezing winds whistled across icy rocks. Giant shards of what looked like crystal stuck up at weird angles. The air was full of dust.

It was so gloomy and dusty that Kip couldn't tell if it was day or night.

'Humans couldn't live here,' said Finbar, his fangs chattering.

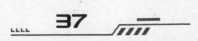

Actually, it looks like NO-ONE lives here, Kip thought. As far as he could tell, Eden-7 was deserted.

'Maybe it's nicer in summer,' Kip said. 'Anyway, our mission is to explore the planet, no matter how terrible it looks.'

'There's a c-c-cave over there,' said Finbar, whose eyesight was excellent.

'Let's shelter there and work out what to do,' Kip said, trying to sound upbeat.

They trudged off.

The wind sliced through Kip's spacesuit like a knife. His spirits slumped.

His first Space Scout mission should have been thrilling. High-tech. Dangerous. Not miserable and cold like this place!

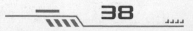

CHAPTER 5

Kip and Finbar reached the cave. It was still freezing cold. But now that they were out of the wind, Kip felt like he was back home under his programmable doona set to 'Tahiti'.

Suddenly, a shrill call echoed through the shadowy cave. It was something between a shiver and a shriek.

Then there was another unmistakable noise. Footsteps were coming towards them from deep inside the cave!

'There's life here after all!' Kip said, feeling excited about the mission again.

'We should hide,' said Finbar. 'We don't know who or what the noises belong to!'

Kip and Finbar ducked into the shadows just in time.

Hundreds of cold, green eyes appeared in the gloom. Moments later, Kip saw who the eyes belonged to.

The creatures came up to Kip's waist and walked on two legs. Thick, spiked tails swished behind them as they ran out of the cave. Kip could hear them calling to

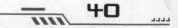

each other in their alien language as they passed by.

In Space Scout training, Kip had learnt how to act when he came across a new kind of alien. Some aliens were friendly and some weren't.

Kip knew he had to be cautious. If these aliens were unfriendly, those spikes and claws could be dangerous.

Secretly, Kip thought battling evil aliens would be pretty cool for a first mission. He crept forward and looked out of the cave.

Outside, the dust clouds had parted. Three tiny, pale suns shone weakly down. The aliens lay flat on their backs in the pitiful sunshine.

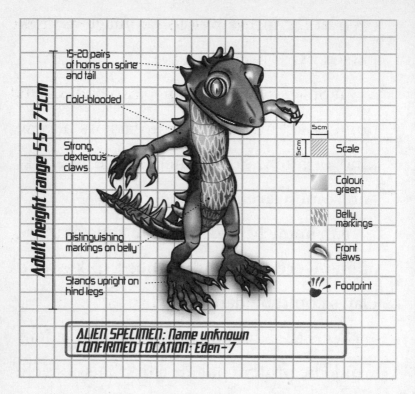

15-20 pairs of horns on spine and tail

Cold-blooded

Strong, dexterous claws

Distinguishing markings on belly

Stands upright on hind legs

Adult height range 55–75cm

5cm

5cm

Scale

Colour: green

Belly markings

Front claws

Footprint

ALIEN SPECIMEN: Name unknown
CONFIRMED LOCATION: Eden-7

They're basking, Kip thought. *Just like Duke does.*

Kip crept back to Finbar. 'I wonder where they came from,' he whispered. 'Maybe underground. If they live below

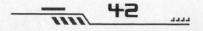

the surface, that would explain how they can survive on this planet.'

'I can hear something,' Finbar whispered suddenly, his super-sensitive wolf ears twitching.

Just then, two new pairs of creepy alien eyes appeared near the roof of the cave. The bigger set of eyes blinked. The eyelids moved from side to side instead of up and down.

It was an alien hanging upside-down from the roof! It jumped down. In the alien's arms was a baby alien.

The baby started wailing, and the mother alien made a soft shivering sound. She rocked the baby alien gently.

'Awww, cute!' said Finbar, reaching out to stroke the baby alien's head.

SCREECH!

The mother alien screeched at Finbar. She ran out of the cave, her baby held tightly in her arms.

'What were you thinking, Finbar?' Kip whispered. 'These aliens aren't cute! They look dangerous.'

He was thinking fast. He had to work out whether humans could live on Eden-7. So far, his hunch that the aliens might live underground was his best bet.

But now the aliens knew Kip and Finbar were there. That meant exploring underground would be a huge risk.

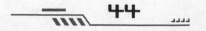

Kip knew what he had to do.

'Let's explore the cave now, while it's empty,' said Kip. 'Those aliens might come back for us at any time!'

Kip paced the cave, trying to work out where the aliens had come from. He followed their footprints in the ice.

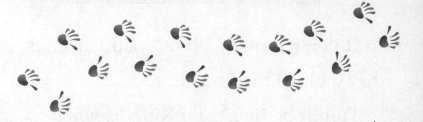

'There's a tunnel at the back of the cave,' said Finbar, pointing to a dark corner.

The tunnel looked big enough for Kip to squeeze through on hands and knees. It would be easier without his helmet on

though. He turned on the air-analyser on his SpaceCuff.

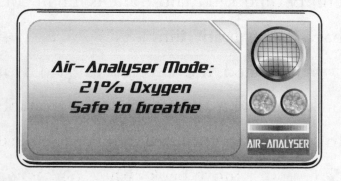

'I don't know if I'll fit,' said Finbar as they took off their helmets.

'You'll be fine,' said Kip, dropping to his knees. He wriggled into the tunnel, backpack in one hand. 'You're 99.9 per cent fluff, aren't you?'

Kip squeezed along the tunnel. It was really only big enough for the aliens to use.

The rocky walls jabbed into Kip's shoulders painfully. He could only move a few centimetres at a time.

'OK back there, Fin?' said Kip. He could twist just enough to see Finbar.

Finbar's wolf tongue panted with exhaustion. He wasn't moving forward. He couldn't move back either. Finbar was stuck!

CHAPTER 6

Kip knew it wasn't Finbar's fault, but they didn't have time for this!

'Those aliens could be back at any moment,' he said, worried.

'I know,' said Finbar grimly. 'I don't fancy meeting those spiky tails in this narrow tunnel, either.' But as hard as he tried, Finbar really couldn't move.

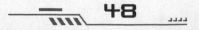

What are we going to do? Kip thought, resting on his backpack. It was stuffed full of all the useless stuff his mum made him pack, like powdered broccoli.

Wait… powdered broccoli!

One of the few interesting things Kip had learnt from his Teacherbots at school was about powdered broccoli.

In the year 2176, scientists discovered

that people who ate powdered broccoli suddenly lost huge amounts of water from their bodies. The effect didn't last long. But the nerdy scientists thought it was because water had been taken out of the broccoli to turn it into a powder.

Whatever the reason, powdered broccoli made people instantly dehydrate and lose weight, since the human body is mostly water.

I wonder if it works on wolves? thought Kip.

He tossed the sachet of powdered broccoli to Finbar, who wrinkled his snout.

'Wolves are meat-eaters!' he said glumly. 'Still, anything for the mission.' He tipped the entire sachet down his throat.

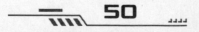

Instantly, clouds of water vapour rose from Finbar's fur. Within seconds, his damp fur was plastered to his face. He looked like a gigantic rat after a bubble bath! But Finbar was now slim enough to squeeze along the tunnel after Kip.

They crawled at top speed for another couple of minutes.

'There's light ahead,' called Kip.

The tunnel widened out and soon Kip could stand. Light was shining weakly through an opening in the rock. Carefully, Kip stepped through.

He gasped. He was on a narrow rock ledge about halfway up the wall of a huge cave. The ledge was only 10 centimetres

wide! He grabbed onto the rock behind him to keep from falling.

The cave was massive. Tunnels like the one Kip had just come through led off in all directions. Pale light filtered through holes in the rocky roof high above.

'What is this place?' asked Finbar, who had stepped onto the ledge next to Kip.

'Maybe the middle of an underground city?' said Kip, thinking aloud. 'We have to explore those tunnels. Humans could live in them… not that I'd want to.'

'We'll have to get off this ledge first,' Finbar replied.

Kip grinned. 'Any good at rock climbing, Fin?'

'None of our ropes are long enough,' said Finbar, level-headed as always.

'Got any dental floss?' said Kip suddenly. *Finbar's teeth are very white,* he thought. *I bet he takes good care of them, even if he is an Animaul.*

Finbar pulled a giant pack of WorldCorp's Microthin Dental Floss from his backpack. He passed it to Kip.

Kip made a loop of dental floss and tied it with a slipknot. He hooked it over a craggy rock.

'Instant safety rope!' grinned Kip. 'Minty-fresh, too.'

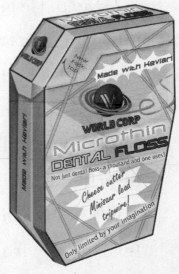

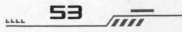

Finbar looked doubtful.

'WorldCorp coats its dental floss with Kevlar,' said Kip. 'It'll hold us, don't worry.'

The nearest tunnel entrance was below them. The climb down would be short but scary. A single thread of dental floss stood between them and a horrific fall.

Kip stepped off the rock ledge, feeling for a toehold. He held onto the dental floss tightly with both hands.

But just as he rested his weight on a hold in the rock, his boot slipped. Rocks tumbled down, falling all the way to the bottom of the cave.

Kip's heart hammered in his chest as he swung away from the rock. He hoped

he wasn't wrong about the dental floss's strength. But it held firm.

Keep going, he thought, reaching back to the rock and steadying his foothold.

This time, Kip didn't slip. He inched his way down the rock wall. Kip was strong and light, but soon his shoulders were burning with the strain.

The climb down was thrilling, but Kip was pleased when it was over. He stepped down onto the floor of the tunnel with a deep sigh of relief.

Kip paused to catch his breath and wait for Finbar. He squinted around. The light through the holes way up in the roof only lit the tunnel a tiny bit.

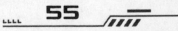

There was a very strange sound in the tunnel, too.

GLUB GLUB GLUB

Ew, Kip thought. *What's that?*

He wasn't sure he wanted to know!

CHAPTER 7

'The walls are covered with bubbles,' said Finbar, stepping down next to Kip. 'And they look like *snot* bubbles.'

Kip flicked on his SpaceCuff. There was no reception underground. But at least the SpaceCuff's light worked.

Holding the SpaceCuff up, Kip peered at the walls. He shuddered. The slimy bubbles

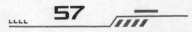

were everywhere!

Inside each was a tiny creature. Suddenly, one burst through its gloopy bubble.

The little creature grabbed the walls with its arms and legs. The way it moved reminded Kip of the mother alien clinging to the roof of the cave.

Suddenly, Kip understood what the gross bubbles were. 'They're alien eggs — with baby aliens inside,' he said. 'This must be some kind of hatchery!'

Finbar reached out and scooped up the hatchling in his paw.

'Don't touch it!' Kip warned.

'It's freezing cold,' said Finbar, ignoring Kip. 'Its lips are blue. Perhaps the babies are too little to handle the cold.'

'Put it down,' said Kip urgently.

Finbar stroked the tiny alien with one furry finger. The creature purred.

'I think the warmth of my paw is helping,' said Finbar.

Kip knew it went against Finbar's

animal instincts to leave a fellow creature in pain. And even if the aliens turned out to be dangerous, he didn't want the babies to freeze either.

But Kip knew they had to get moving. They needed to explore the planet properly, before the aliens came back. Otherwise Kip would fail his first mission, which would be seriously embarrassing.

'We don't know anything about alien first aid,' said Kip. 'We could do more harm than good.'

'I guess you're ri—' Finbar began.

Before he could finish, a chilling sound filled the cave.

SCREECH!

Scuttling aliens appeared from nowhere, thumping their spiked tails. The aliens were short, but their strange scaly bodies seemed to fill the cave.

'Put the baby down!' Kip yelled to Finbar. 'We've got to run!'

Finbar stooped down and gently put the baby alien on a rock.

'Bye, little guy,' said Finbar, giving the baby one last stroke.

'Finbar! Come ON!' Kip yelled, moving into a nearby tunnel.

But it was too late. The aliens had completely surrounded Finbar! There were hundreds of them, and they looked upset.

I've got to save Finbar! Kip thought.

But there were too many aliens. He knew he couldn't do anything if the aliens captured him too.

Kip could only think of one way out. MoNa's Scrambler Beam might just be powerful enough to reach through the holes in the roof and beam Finbar to safety.

It would use a lot of MoNa's energy, but Kip knew it was his best shot of saving Finbar. The only problem was that he didn't want to explain everything to his starship.

MoNa already thinks she knows more than I do, Kip thought. *What's she going to think when I ask her to save us?*

Still, he didn't have much choice. *Got to*

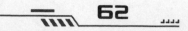

get to the surface and call MoNa, he thought.

But before Kip started heading up, he pulled a Stick-E-Cam from his backpack.

STICK!
CLICK!
PERFECT
PIC!

Sticky back

Paper-thin

Stick-E-Cams were super-thin cameras disguised as ordinary stickers. Kip's SpaceCuff could connect to any nearby Stick-E-Cam via bluetooth.

Kip plastered the Stick-E-Cam to the wall of the tunnel. Now Kip could keep watch on the tunnel from the surface while he worked out how to rescue Finbar.

Once Kip had tested the position of the Stick-E-Cam, he felt his way along the rocky wall of the dim tunnel.

Those aliens couldn't have come from nowhere, Kip reasoned. *This tunnel must lead to the surface.*

The tunnel sloped steeply upwards, so Kip figured he was right.

Getting down on his hands and knees, Kip crawled up through the tunnel as fast as he could. The rocky ground jabbed into his knees through his ultra-light spacesuit, but Kip barely noticed.

Finbar's counting on me, Kip thought, *and I won't let him down.*

After an exhausting crawl, Kip finally

saw weak sunlight up ahead. *I was right!* he thought, his mood soaring. *The tunnel leads to the surface.*

He slapped on his helmet and attached his OxyGlobe again. The air on the surface was so dusty that it wouldn't be safe to breathe.

Kip scrambled towards the light. A second later, he was on the bitterly cold surface of Eden-7. He was in the middle of the massive crater he'd seen from space.

Turning on his SpaceCuff, Kip linked into the Stick-E-Cam on the cave wall.

Straight away, he wished he hadn't. He didn't like what was going on in the tunnel.

Not at *all*.

CHAPTER 8

In the weak light of the cave, Kip could just make out Finbar's fluffy shape on his SpaceCuff screen.

It looked like the alien hatchlings were swarming all over him. He was covered in baby aliens!

Hatchlings nestled in Finbar's furry

arms, on his shoulders and even on his head!

A theory popped into Kip's mind.

The hatchlings are cold and sick. Finbar's all warm and furry. Maybe the aliens are using Finbar as a giant, walking heat source!

Kip remembered how evil the aliens had seemed. Now he wondered if he was wrong about them.

They looked and behaved differently to him. But they were only doing what they had to do to survive – just like Kip.

Just then, Kip noticed a message flashing on his SpaceCuff. It was an old message. Kip hadn't received it because there was no reception that far underground in the tunnels.

SENDER: MoNa 4000
SUBJECT: Return to ship immediately.

The Eden-7 atmosphere is so cold that my fuel is freezing. Even my anti-freeze is freezing. Heating has nearly used all my energy reserves. Soon I won't have enough power for two Scrambler Beams.

I'll have to leave you stranded.

Surely MoNa wouldn't really do that? thought Kip, horrified. MoNa was supposed to help and protect him.

But she did have a terrible habit of thinking she knew best. *Imagine being stuck in this horrible frozen wasteland forever*, he shuddered.

Basking desperately for any shred of

heat like the aliens did. Caring for freezing alien hatchlings. Every day, looking at that horrible giant meteorite scar…

That meteorite must have been bigger than the one that killed the dinosaurs on Earth, Kip thought. Dinosaurs (and other extinct animals like pigs and budgies) were a personal interest of Kip's.

Kip knew exactly how the giant meteorite had killed Earth's dinosaurs. When it fell, it caused so much dust that it blocked the sun. Earth was plunged into a massive, deadly ice age.

Suddenly the pieces fell into place. *That's exactly what's happening on Eden-7!* Kip thought.

It made perfect sense. Until the meteorite hit, Eden-7 had been warm, just as WorldCorp predicted. But now the planet was unbearably cold.

If a massive ice age is coming here, the temperature will have dropped since the last time I checked, Kip decided.

Sure enough, the temperature gauge on Kip's SpaceCuff read 346 degrees below zero. 30 degrees lower than before! And heavy snow clouds were massing in the sky.

Kip was sure he was right. The ice age was coming. Fast! If MoNa left Kip and Finbar stranded, it would kill them for sure.

Kip knew they had to leave Eden-7 urgently. But there was no way his plan to rescue Finbar would work. MoNa would need extra energy to shine a Scrambler Beam through the roof of a cave. She might not even have enough energy for a normal Scrambler Beam.

This is not how I thought my first Space Scout mission would turn out, Kip thought.

He wanted the mission to be a glittering success. He'd discover a perfect planet, solve Earth's problems and meet some cool, super-advanced aliens along the way.

The aliens here are so primitive, Kip grouched. *They don't even know basic things, like keeping warm with fire!*

Fire.

Kip turned the word over in his mind. An idea blossomed. It was so simple! Why hadn't he thought of it before?

Kip's hand closed around WorldCorp's Interplanetary Emergency Kit stashed in his backpack. He ran through the contents.

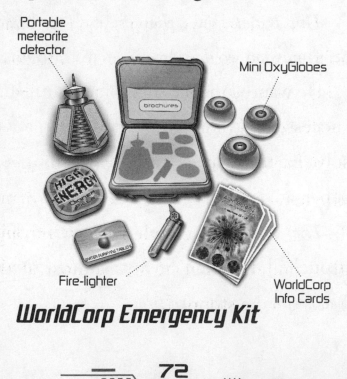

Portable meteorite detector

Mini OxyGlobes

brochures

HIGH ENERGY DINNER PILLS

WATER PURIFYING TABLETS

Fire-lighter

WorldCorp Info Cards

WorldCorp Emergency Kit

Water-purifying tablets. High-energy dinner pills. And, most important of all, a tiny laser fire-lighter.

Kip could introduce the aliens to fire. Then they'd have an endless heat source. There'd be no need to keep Finbar prisoner!

Crouching down, Kip ripped up a bunch of frozen weeds poking out of the rock. The weeds were leathery, blue and dry.

Perfect, he thought.

Kip raced into the tunnel leading to the hatchery. Clutching the weeds firmly in one hand, he crawled down through the tunnel. When he was almost at the hatchery, he stopped.

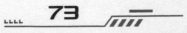

He took the lighter from the kit. His hands trembling, Kip clicked the ignition button on the lighter. The laser fired, but nothing else happened.

With a sickening feeling, Kip realised that the lighter wasn't as heavy as it should have been.

A shiver of fear ran up and down Kip's spine. The lighter's fuel was really low.

He gave it a shake. *Please let this work,* he thought. *Everything depends on this lighter!*

CHAPTER 9

Kip took a deep breath. He clicked the ignition button again.

There was a hissing sound, and a moment later the flame flared. *Yes!*

Carefully, Kip cupped his free hand around the flame so it wouldn't go out.

Kip held the flame to the bunch of blue weeds. The edge of the weeds began to

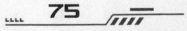

smoke and soon the entire bundle was a roaring ball of flames.

But Kip knew he was only halfway there. His whole plan depended on the aliens not being dangerous after all. Kip hoped he was right that the aliens only wanted to protect their babies.

Tossing the flaming ball from hand to hand, Kip raced into the hatchery. *Lucky for flame-proof space gloves*, he thought.

'Hello,' Kip said, as loudly and politely as he could. 'I need with speak to you!'

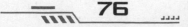

Finbar was still covered in hatchlings. Seeing Kip with the flame ball, his mouth dropped open.

The aliens stared at Kip too. But no-one tried to grab or capture him. They were frozen to the spot.

Pointing to the flaming weeds in Kip's hand, the nearest alien stepped forward. Kip saw that it had a baby on its back.

Looks like the alien we saw in the cave, thought Kip.

Curious, the mother alien held a claw up to the flame. Her eyes boggled in amazement.

'Don't touch it!' Kip warned.

Too late! Yelping, the alien snatched her

claw back. Blisters were already forming on her scaly skin. Kip remembered then that the aliens didn't speak English.

Luckily, being an Animaul meant that Finbar's specialty was understanding other creatures' languages.

'I've picked up a few words of their language,' Finbar said. 'You talk, and I'll translate.'

Kip nodded, and took a deep breath. 'OK. Aliens, I am showing you how to make fire,' he began. He placed the weed ball down and held his hands up to it. 'Warm yourselves like this and you will survive the ice age.'

Finbar translated Kip's speech as best he

could. Kip wasn't sure it was coming out very well, but the aliens were listening.

The aliens gathered around the flame ball. Following Kip's example, they held up their claws to the heat. A pleased whispering filled the cave. Kip showed them how to feed the fire with more weeds and cup their claws around the flame to make sure it didn't go out.

'So now you don't need my friend to keep your hatchlings warm,' Kip said.

Gently, Kip scooped the tiny alien hatchlings from Finbar's fur. Their scales were soft, smooth and freezing cold to touch. As Kip put them gently down on the ground, their wriggling legs tickled his

hands. The aliens picked up their hatchlings and warmed them by the fire.

'We are going to leave your planet now,' Kip said.

Kip felt something pressing on the leg of his spacesuit. He looked down. An alien hatchling was patting Kip's leg – almost as though it was thanking him. Kip looked down and smiled at the scaly creature.

He felt a lump in his throat. Then he shook his head. *Snap out of it, Kip!* he told himself. *You're becoming as soft as Finbar!*

Finbar was tickling one of the hatchlings under the chin.

'Hurry, Finbar!' said Kip. 'MoNa's energy reserves are dangerously low. If we

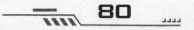

don't get out of here soon, she'll leave us behind.'

Finbar nodded. Kip could tell that even though Finbar liked the hatchlings, he didn't want to be a living heater for the rest of his life.

Finbar inched backwards out of the hatchery, with Kip close behind. The aliens were so pleased with the fire, they let Kip and Finbar go without a fuss.

'The surface is this way,' said Kip, pointing to the tunnel he came through earlier. Finbar's ears flattened against his head.

'Don't worry,' Kip said. 'This one's way bigger than the first one.'

Kip and Finbar crawled through the tunnel as fast as they could. They didn't want to stay on Eden-7 any longer than they had to.

They sped out of the tunnel and onto the surface. Immediately, Kip called MoNa on his SpaceCuff.

'Kirby to MoNa,' he said urgently.

'MoNa… receeeeeivvvvinnngggg…' MoNa said sleepily.

'Send two Scrambler Beams right away!' Kip said.

'Has she got enough power?' asked Finbar in a worried voice.

'I'm sure she does,' said Kip, sounding more confident than he felt.

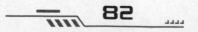

They waited for
a tense moment,
staring into the
sky. Then two
pale, weak beams broke through the dust
clouds.

Kip and Finbar stepped into the beams.
Kip had the familiar feeling that he was
being poked by thousands of tiny pins.
Only this time, the pins felt slower and
weaker. Kip's feet lifted off the ground, but
his particles didn't separate
as quickly as usual. He was
rising into the air, ever so
slowly.

Then, with a sickening

lurch, Kip dropped almost to the ground again.

Come on, MoNa, Kip silently begged.

Again, Kip felt himself rising. There was the tingling feeling in his arms and legs, and…

A second later, Kip opened his eyes. He was back in MoNa's landing bay, dazed and blinking. Finbar lay curled into a ball beside him.

They'd made it back — but only just.

CHAPTER 10

With her last shred of energy, MoNa fired her thrusters and sped out of Eden-7's orbit.

Kip and Finbar picked themselves up, tore off their helmets and left the landing bay. On the way through the shining circular door, Kip caught sight of his reflection.

His spacesuit was grey with dust.

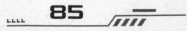

His sweaty hair lay flat against his head.

'I hate helmet hair!' Kip muttered. 'I need a shower.'

'Me too,' said Finbar, whose fur was brown and matted. 'I'll show you where they are.'

Kip followed Finbar to a gleaming silver door labelled 'Bubble Showers'. He stepped into one cubicle and Finbar into another.

Kip's cubicle was a glowing blue chamber with a plughole in the floor. Jets were fixed to the roof. On one wall Kip saw a pair of taps.

Kip stepped out of his clothes and turned the taps on hard.

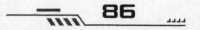

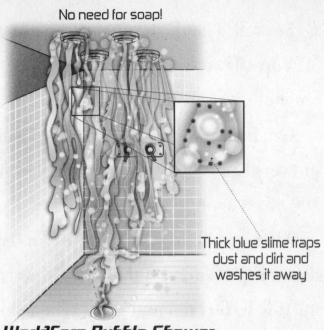

No need for soap!

Thick blue slime traps dust and dirt and washes it away

WorldCorp Bubble Shower

Thick blue slime spurted from the jets on the roof.

That's better, Kip thought, standing underneath. The slime oozed onto his hair and skin. It formed bubbles that rolled down his arms and back, picking up dust

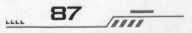

as they fell. The dusty slime bubbles rolled off Kip's feet and disappeared down the plughole.

On Earth, water was scarce. Bubble showers had replaced water showers about 200 years ago.

After a relaxing 10 minutes under the slime, Kip turned off the taps. He was just starting to feel normal again when a bossy voice interrupted him.

'Don't dawdle in the shower!' MoNa snapped. 'You've got a report to file.'

She even tries to boss me around in the shower, Kip grumbled to himself.

As soon as MoNa had left Eden-7's freezing atmosphere, her fuel started

thawing. She was full of energy again.

After putting on a clean spacesuit, Kip walked to the bridge.

When he got there, he found Finbar waiting for him. Finbar was as fluffy as a hybrid kitten-rabbit after his shower.

Kip settled into his captain's chair. He woke the holographic consol and touched the Captain's Log button.

The floating holographic keyboard appeared in front of Kip's hands. He typed up his report and then clicked Send.

Kip settled back on his captain's chair. His first mission would earn him one Planetary Point. Not ideal, but not embarrassing either.

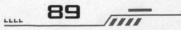

CAPTAIN'S LOG
Eden-7

Climate: A rocky planet in the Mega Meteor Galaxy. I believe that Eden-7 was once warm, as WorldCorp predicted. But now Eden-7 is about to go into a killer ice age. Likely cause is a giant meteor strike.

Population: Lizard-like scaly creatures, which seemed dangerous at first. Later we learnt the creatures were just struggling to survive.

National pastimes: Sunbaking, rock climbing.

Summary: The aliens aren't dangerous, but I still don't recommend Eden-7 as an alternative to Earth. It is too cold. WorldCorp would have to invent super heavy-duty thermal underwear first.

KIP KIRBY, SPACE SCOUT #50

Space Scouts earned one Planetary Point for a completed mission and two for a promising discovery. The points were tallied up on the intranet's Leader Board.

'Do you think the aliens will be OK?' said Finbar.

'Yes, because they're small,' Kip replied. 'When Earth was hit by a meteorite, the big animals died out. The smaller ones lived.'

Finbar looked relieved. 'And now that they can keep warm, they should be fine.'

Kip smiled. Finbar was so soft! He was definitely *not* your average Animaul.

But that was fine, because Kip was not your average Space Scout.

THE END